GW00457054

Trombone
Scales & Exercises

for Trinity College London
Treble Clef & Bass Clef
Trombone examinations
from 2007

Grades 1–8

Published by
Trinity College London

Registered Office:
4th floor, 89 Albert Embankment
London SE1 7TP UK

T +44 (0)20 7820 6100
F +44 (0)20 7820 6161
E music@trinitycollege.co.uk
www.trinitycollege.co.uk

Registered in the UK
Company no. 02683033
Charity no. 1014792

Treble Clef
Grade 1

Candidate to prepare one lip flexibility exercise and then *either* Section i) *or* Section ii) in full:

Lip Flexibility Exercise:

No. 1 Ascending and descending

♩= *c.* 86   Play this exercise legato, using the slide positions given.

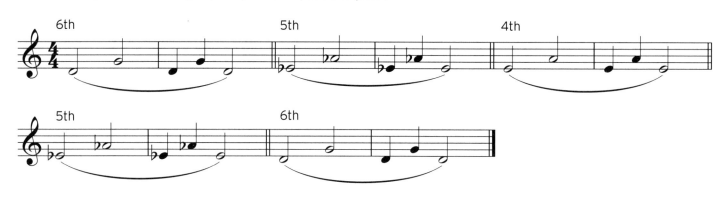

or

No. 2 Descending and ascending

♩= *c.* 86   Play this exercise legato, using the slide positions given.

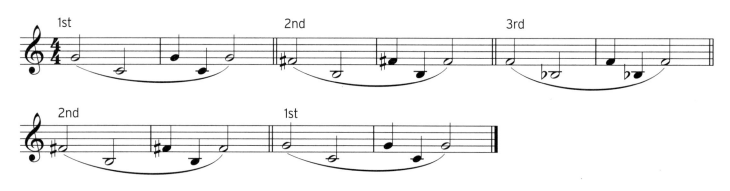

either i) **Scales and Arpeggios (from memory):**

The following scales and arpeggios to be performed **_mf_** and tongued (♩ = 46-60):

C major scale (one octave)

C major arpeggio (one octave)

A natural minor scale (one octave)

Alternatively, candidates may play the harmonic or melodic form of the minor, as follows:

A harmonic minor scale (one octave)

or

A melodic minor scale (one octave)

A minor arpeggio (one octave)

or ii) **Exercise:**

The following exercise to be performed tongued (♩ = 46-60):

C major scale and arpeggio exercise

Grade 2

Candidate to prepare one lip flexibility exercise and then *either* Section i) *or* Section ii) in full:

Lip Flexibility Exercise:

No. 1 Ascending and descending

♩ = c. 92   Play this exercise legato, using the slide positions given.

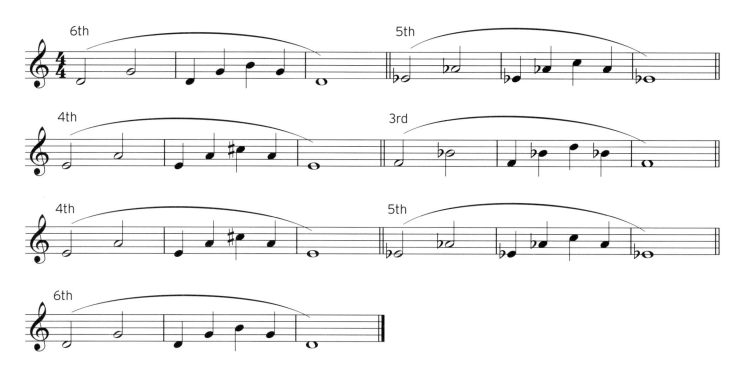

or

No. 2 Descending and ascending

♩ = c. 80   Play this exercise legato, using the slide positions given.

either i) **Scales and Arpeggios (from memory):**

The following scales and arpeggios to be performed ***mf*** and tongued (♩ = 50-66):

D major scale (one octave)

D major arpeggio (one octave)

A harmonic minor scale (one octave)

Alternatively, candidates may play the natural or melodic form of the minor, as follows:

A natural minor scale (one octave)

or

A melodic minor scale (one octave)

A minor arpeggio (one octave)

B♭ major scale (one octave)

B♭ major arpeggio (one octave)

Grade 2 continued

or ii) **Exercises:**

The following exercises to be performed tongued (♩ = 50-66):

D major scale and arpeggio exercise

A minor scale and arpeggio exercise

Grade 3

Candidate to prepare one lip flexibility exercise and then *either* Section i) *or* Section ii) in full:

Lip Flexibility Exercise:

No. 1 Ascending and descending

♩= c. 92   Play this exercise legato, using the slide positions given.

or

No. 2 Descending and ascending

♩= c. 92   Play this exercise legato, using the slide positions given.

Grade 3 continued

either i) **Scales and Arpeggios (from memory):**

The following scales and arpeggios to be performed ***mf*** and tongued (♩ = 54-72):

D harmonic minor scale (one octave)

or

D melodic minor scale (one octave)

D minor arpeggio (one octave)

E major scale (one octave)

E major arpeggio (one octave)

E harmonic minor scale (one octave)

or

E melodic minor scale (one octave)

E minor arpeggio (one octave)

F major scale (one octave)

F major arpeggio (one octave)

or ii) **Exercises:**

The following exercises to be performed tongued (♩ = 54-72):

D minor scale and arpeggio exercise

E major scale and arpeggio exercise

F major scale and arpeggio exercise

Grade 4

Candidate to prepare one lip flexibility exercise and then *either* Section i) *or* Section ii) in full:

Lip Flexibility Exercise:

No. 1 Ascending and descending

♩ = c. 92   Play this exercise legato, using the slide positions given.

Repeat using the following slide positions:

3rd – 2nd – 1st – 2nd – 3rd – 4th

or

No. 2 Descending and ascending

♩ = c. 92   Play this exercise legato, using the slide positions given.

Repeat using the following slide positions:

2nd – 3rd – 4th – 3rd – 2nd – 1st

either i) **Scales and Arpeggios (from memory):**

The following scales and arpeggios to be performed ***mf***; tongued *or* legato tongued as requested by the examiner
(♩ = 60-104):

C harmonic minor scale (one octave)

or

C melodic minor scale (one octave)

C minor arpeggio (one octave)

Chromatic scale starting on D (one octave)

Whole-tone scale starting on D (one octave)

E♭ major scale (one octave)

E♭ major arpeggio (one octave)

F♯ harmonic minor scale (one octave)

or

F♯ melodic minor scale (one octave)

F♯ minor arpeggio (one octave)

B♭ major scale (to 12th)

B♭ major arpeggio (to 12th)

Grade 4 continued

or ii) **Exercises:**

The following exercises to be performed *either* tongued *or* including legato as indicated, as requested by the examiner (♩ = 60-104):

C minor expanding scale exercise

E♭ major expanding scale exercise

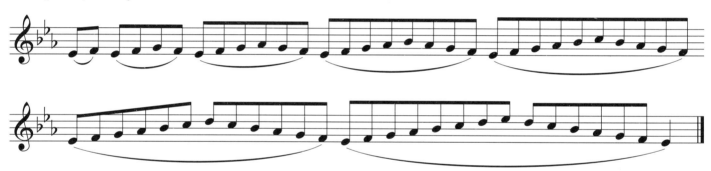

B♭ major scale and arpeggio exercise

Grade 5

Candidate to prepare one lip flexibility exercise and then *either* Section i) *or* Section ii) in full:

Lip Flexibility Exercise:

No. 1 Ascending

♩ = *c.* 120   Play this exercise legato, using the slide positions given.

Repeat using the following slide positions:

5th – 4th – 3rd – 2nd – 1st

or

No. 2 Descending

♩ = *c.* 120   Play this exercise legato, using the slide positions given.

Repeat using the following slide positions:

2nd – 3rd – 4th – 5th – 6th

either i) **Scales and Arpeggios (from memory):**

The following scales and arpeggios to be performed ***mf***; tongued *or* legato tongued as requested by the examiner
(♩ = 60-104):

G major scale (two octaves)

G major arpeggio (two octaves)

Grade 5 continued

G harmonic minor scale (two octaves)

or

G melodic minor scale (two octaves)

G minor arpeggio (two octaves)

Chromatic scale starting on G (two octaves)

Whole-tone scale starting on G (two octaves)

Dominant 7th in the key of G (one octave)*

*If preferred, the dominant 7th may be finished on the starting note rather than resolving onto the tonic.

B major scale (to 12th)

B major arpeggio (to 12th)

B harmonic minor scale (to 12th)

or

B melodic minor scale (to 12th)

B minor arpeggio (to 12th)

or ii) **Exercises:**

The following exercises to be performed *either* tongued *or* including legato as indicated, as requested by the examiner
(♩ = 66-112):

B major scale and arpeggio exercise

Grade 5 continued

B minor scale and arpeggio exercise

G major expanding scale exercise

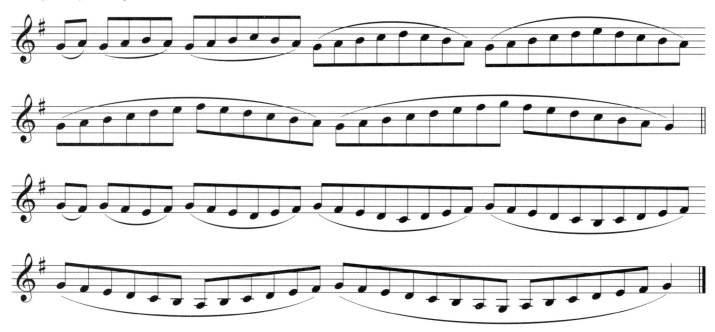

G minor expanding scale exercise

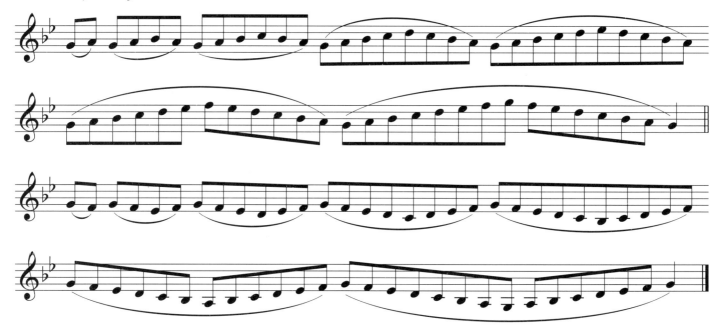

Grade 6

Candidate to prepare one lip flexibility exercise and then *either* Section i) *or* Section ii) in full:

Lip Flexibility Exercise:

No. 1 Ascending

♩= c. 160   Play this exercise legato, using the slide positions given.

Repeat using the following slide positions:

5th − 4th − 3rd − 2nd − 1st

or

No. 2 Descending

♩= c. 60   Play this exercise legato, using the slide positions given.

Repeat using the following slide positions:

2nd − 3rd − 4th − 5th − 6th

either i) **Scales and Arpeggios (from memory):**

The following scales and arpeggios to be performed *f* or *p*, tongued *or* legato tongued as requested by the examiner
(♩ = 72-120):

F♯ major scale (two octaves)

F♯ major arpeggio (two octaves)

Grade 6 continued

F# harmonic minor scale (two octaves)

F# melodic minor scale (two octaves)

F# minor arpeggio (two octaves)

A major scale (two octaves)

A major arpeggio (two octaves)

A harmonic minor scale (two octaves)

A melodic minor scale (two octaves)

A minor arpeggio (two octaves)

Chromatic scale starting on A (two octaves)

Whole-tone scale starting on A (two octaves)

Augmented arpeggio starting on A (two octaves)

Dominant 7th in the key of A (one octave)*

Diminished 7th starting on A (two octaves)

*If preferred, the dominant 7th may be finished on the starting note rather than resolving onto the tonic.

Grade 6 continued

or ii) **Exercises:**

The following exercises to be performed *either* tongued *or* including legato as indicated, as requested by the examiner
(♩ = 72–120):

Key centre exercise in A

A major expanding scale exercise

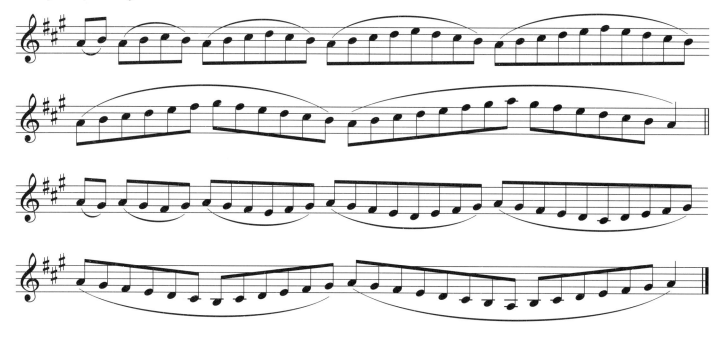

A major scale in thirds

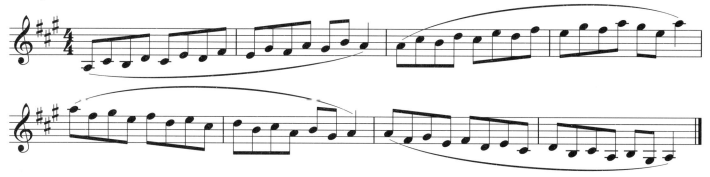

A minor expanding scale exercise

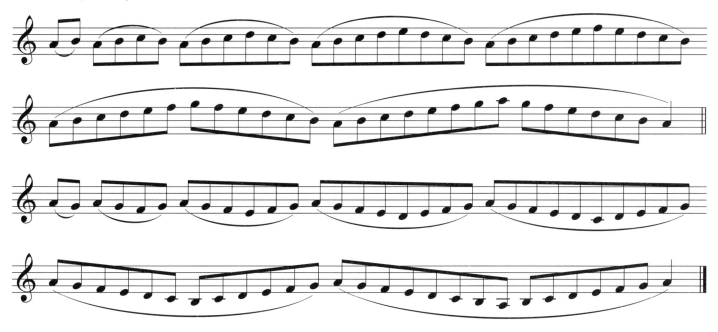

A minor scale in thirds

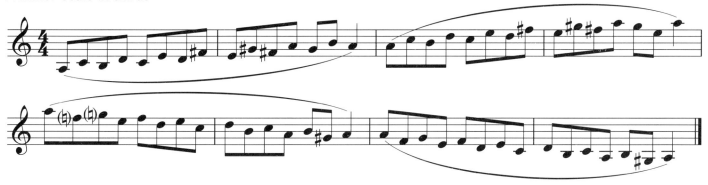

Grade 7

Candidate to prepare one lip flexibility exercise and then *either* Section i) *or* Section ii) in full:

Lip Flexibility Exercise:

No. 1 Ascending

♩ = *c*. 160   Play this exercise legato, using the slide positions given.

Repeat using the following slide positions:

5th – 4th – 3rd – 2nd

or

No. 2 Descending

♩ = *c*. 92   Play this exercise legato, using the slide positions given.

Repeat using the following slide positions:

2nd – 3rd – 4th – 5th – 6th

either i) **Scales and Arpeggios (from memory):**

The following scales and arpeggios to be performed $\boldsymbol{f}$ *or* $\boldsymbol{p}$, tongued *or* legato tongued as requested by the examiner ($\quarternote$ = 80-126):

B♭ major scale (two octaves)

B♭ major arpeggio (two octaves)

B♭ harmonic minor scale (two octaves)

B♭ melodic minor scale (two octaves)

B♭ minor arpeggio (two octaves)

Chromatic scale starting on B♭ (two octaves)

Whole-tone scale starting on B♭ (two octaves)

Grade 7 continued

Augmented arpeggio starting on B♭ (two octaves)

Dominant 7th in the key of B♭ (one octave)*

Diminished 7th starting on B♭ (two octaves)

B major scale (two octaves)

B major arpeggio (two octaves)

B harmonic minor scale (two octaves)

B melodic minor scale (two octaves)

B minor arpeggio (two octaves)

*If preferred, the dominant 7th may be finished on the starting note rather than resolving onto the tonic.

Chromatic scale starting on B (two octaves)

Whole-tone scale starting on B (two octaves)

Augmented arpeggio starting on B (two octaves)

Dominant 7th in the key of B (one octave)*

Diminished 7th starting on B (two octaves)

*If preferred, the dominant 7th may be finished on the starting note rather than resolving onto the tonic.

Grade 7 continued

or ii) **Exercises:**

The following exercises to be performed *either* tongued *or* including legato as indicated, as requested by the examiner (♩ = 80-126):

Key centre exercise in B♭

B♭ major expanding scale exercise

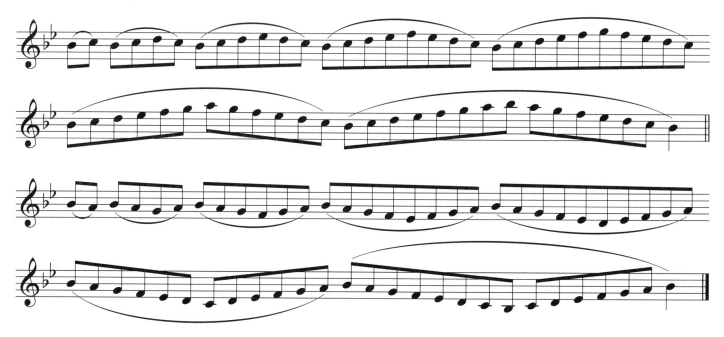

B♭ minor scale in thirds

B major scale in thirds

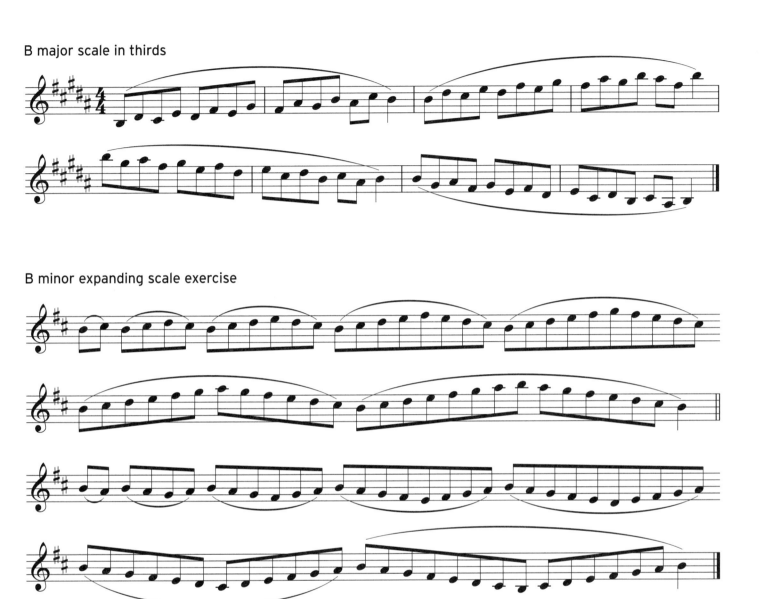

B minor expanding scale exercise

Grade 8

Candidate to prepare one lip flexibility exercise and then *either* Section i) *or* Section ii) in full:

Lip Flexibility Exercise:

No. 1 Ascending

♩ = c. 92   Play this exercise legato, using the slide positions given.

Repeat using the following slide positions:

5th − 4th − 3rd − 2nd − 1st

or

No. 2 Descending

♩ = c. 92   Play this exercise legato, using the slide positions given.

Repeat using the following slide positions:

2nd − 3rd − 4th − 5th − 6th

either i) Scales and Arpeggios (from memory):

The following scales and arpeggios to be performed *f* or *p*, tongued *or* legato tongued *or* legato tongued in pairs (scales only) as requested by the examiner. (♩ = 88-132)

C major scale (two octaves)

C major arpeggio (two octaves)

C harmonic minor scale (two octaves)

C melodic minor scale (two octaves)

C minor arpeggio (two octaves)

Chromatic scale starting on C (two octaves)

Whole-tone scale starting on C (two octaves)

Augmented arpeggio starting on C (two octaves)

Dominant 7th in the key of C (two octaves)*

*If preferred, the dominant 7th may be finished on the starting note rather than resolving onto the tonic.

Grade 8 continued

Diminished 7th starting on C (two octaves)

F# major scale (two octaves)

F# major arpeggio (two octaves)

F# harmonic minor scale (two octaves)

F# melodic minor scale (two octaves)

F# minor arpeggio (two octaves)

Chromatic scale starting on F# (two octaves)

Whole-tone scale starting on F♯ (two octaves)

Augmented arpeggio starting on F♯ (two octaves)

Dominant 7th in the key of F♯ (one octave)*

Diminished 7th starting on F♯ (two octaves)

A♭ major scale (two octaves)

A♭ major arpeggio (two octaves)

G♯/A♭ harmonic minor scale (two octaves)

*If preferred, the dominant 7th may be finished on the starting note rather than resolving onto the tonic.

Grade 8 continued

G#/A♭ melodic minor scale (two octaves)

G#/A♭ minor arpeggio (two octaves)

Chromatic scale starting on A♭ (two octaves)

Whole-tone scale starting on A♭ (two octaves)

Augmented arpeggio starting on A♭ (two octaves)

Dominant 7th in the key of A♭ (one octave)*

Diminished 7th starting on A♭ (two octaves)

*If preferred, the dominant 7th may be finished on the starting note rather than resolving onto the tonic.

Crabwise scale from C (two octaves – tongued *or* legato as indicated)

Crabwise scale from G (two octaves – tongued *or* legato as indicated)

Grade 8 continued

or ii) **Exercises:**

The following exercises to be performed either tongued or including legato as indicated, as requested by the examiner
(♩ = 88-132):

Key centre exercise in C

Key centre exercise in F♯

Key centre exercise in A♭

Crabwise scale from G in thirds

Bass Clef
Grade 1

Candidate to prepare one lip flexibility exercise and then *either* Section i) *or* Section ii) in full:

Lip Flexibility Exercise:

No. 1 Ascending and descending

♩ = *c.* 86   Play this exercise legato, using the slide positions given.

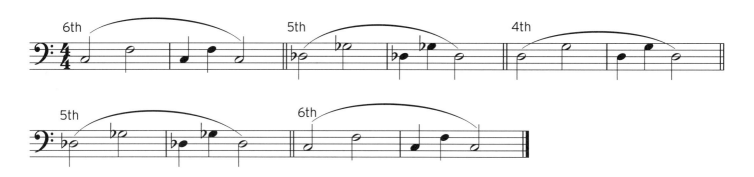

or

No. 2 Descending and ascending

♩ = *c.* 86   Play this exercise legato, using the slide positions given.

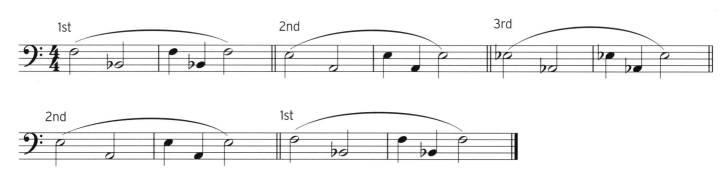

either i) **Scales and Arpeggios (from memory):**

The following scales and arpeggios to be performed *mf* and tongued (♩ = 46-60):

B♭ major scale (one octave)

B♭ major arpeggio (one octave)

G natural minor scale (one octave)

Alternatively, candidates may play the harmonic *or* melodic form of the minor, as follows:

G harmonic minor scale (one octave)

or

G melodic minor scale (one octave)

G minor arpeggio (one octave)

or ii) **Exercises:**

The following exercise to be performed tongued (♩ = 46-60):

B♭ major scale and arpeggio exercise

Grade 2

Candidate to prepare one lip flexibility exercise and then *either* Section i) *or* Section ii) in full:

Lip Flexibility Exercise:

No. 1 Ascending and descending

♩ = c. 92   Play this exercise legato, using the slide positions given.

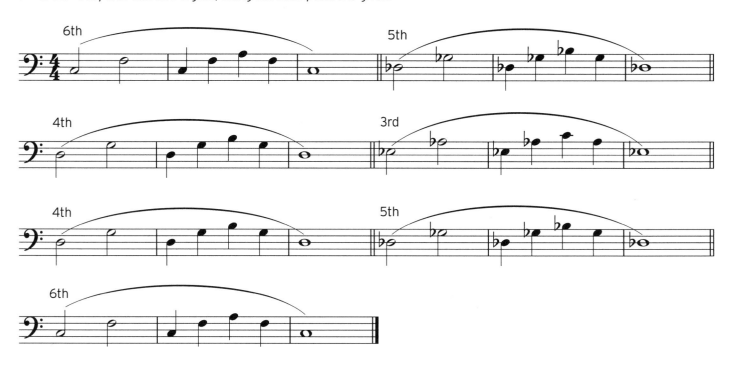

or

No. 2 Descending and ascending

♩ = c. 80   Play this exercise legato, using the slide positions given.

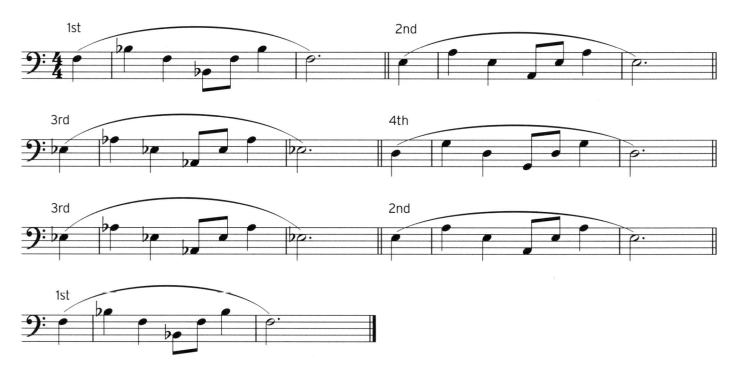

either i) **Scales and Arpeggios (from memory):**

The following scales and arpeggios to be performed *mf* and tongued (♩ = 50-66):

C major scale (one octave)

C major arpeggio (one octave)

G harmonic minor scale (one octave)

Alternatively, candidates may play the natural *or* melodic form of the minor, as follows:

G natural minor scale (one octave)

or

G melodic minor scale (one octave)

G minor arpeggio (one octave)

A♭ major scale (one octave)

A♭ major arpeggio (one octave)

Grade 2 continued

or ii) **Exercises:**

The following exercises to be performed tongued (♩ = 50-66):

C major scale and arpeggio exercise

G minor scale and arpeggio exercise

Grade 3

Candidate to prepare one lip flexibility exercise and then *either* Section i) *or* Section ii) in full:

Lip Flexibility Exercise:

No. 1 Ascending and descending

♩ = c. 92   Play this exercise legato, using the slide positions given.

or

No. 2 Descending and ascending

♩ = c. 92   Play this exercise legato, using the slide positions given.

Grade 3 continued

either i) Scales and Arpeggios (from memory):

The following scales and arpeggios to be performed **mf** and tongued (♩ = 54-72):

C harmonic minor scale (one octave)

or

C melodic minor scale (one octave)

C minor arpeggio (one octave)

D major scale (one octave)

D major arpeggio (one octave)

D harmonic minor scale (one octave)

or

D melodic minor scale (one octave)

D minor arpeggio (one octave)

Eb major scale (one octave)

Eb major arpeggio (one octave)

or ii) **Exercises:**

The following exercises to be performed tongued (♩ = 54-72):

C minor scale and arpeggio exercise

D major scale and arpeggio exercise

Eb major scale and arpeggio exercise

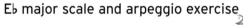

Grade 4

Candidate to prepare one lip flexibility exercise and then *either* Section i) *or* Section ii) in full:

Lip Flexibility Exercise:

No. 1 Ascending and descending

♩ = c. 92   Play this exercise legato, using the slide positions given.

Repeat using the following slide positions:

3rd – 2nd – 1st – 2nd – 3rd – 4th

or

No. 2 Descending and ascending

♩ = c. 92   Play this exercise legato, using the slide positions given.

Repeat using the following slide positions:

2nd – 3rd – 4th – 3rd – 2nd – 1st

either i) Scales and Arpeggios (from memory):

The following scales and arpeggios to be performed ***mf*** and *either* tongued *or* legato tongued as requested by the examiner (♩ = 60-104):

B♭ harmonic minor scale (one octave)

B♭ melodic minor scale (one octave)

B♭ minor arpeggio (one octave)

Chromatic scale starting on C (one octave)

Whole-tone scale starting on C (one octave)

D♭ major scale (one octave)

D♭ major arpeggio (one octave)

E harmonic minor scale (one octave)

or

E melodic minor scale (one octave)

E minor arpeggio (one octave)

A♭ major scale (to 12th)

A♭ major arpeggio (to 12th)

Grade 4 continued

or ii) **Exercises:**

The following exercises to be performed *either* tongued *or* including legato as indicated, as requested by the examiner (♩ = 60-104):

B♭ minor expanding scale exercise

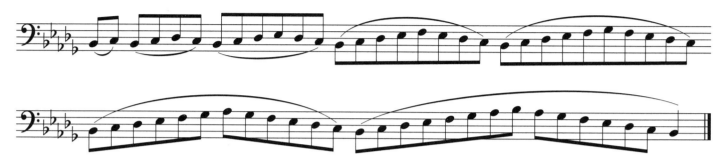

D♭ major expanding scale exercise

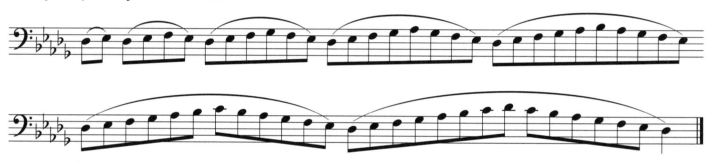

A♭ major scale and arpeggio exercise

Grade 5

Candidate to prepare one lip flexibility exercise and then *either* Section i) *or* Section ii) in full:

Lip Flexibility Exercise:

No. 1 Ascending

♩ = *c.* 120   Play this exercise legato, using the slide positions given.

Repeat using the following slide positions:

5th − 4th − 3rd − 2nd − 1st

or

No. 2 Descending

♩ = *c.* 120   Play this exercise legato, using the slide positions given.

Repeat using the following slide positions:

2nd − 3rd − 4th − 5th − 6th

either i) **Scales and Arpeggios (from memory):**

The following scales and arpeggios to be performed *mf*; tongued *or* legato tongued as requested by the examiner (♩ = 60–104):

F major scale (two octaves)

F major arpeggio (two octaves)

Grade 5 continued

F harmonic minor scale (two octaves)

or

F melodic minor scale (two octaves)

F minor arpeggio (two octaves)

Chromatic scale starting on F (two octaves)

Whole-tone scale starting on F (two octaves)

Dominant 7th in the key of F (one octave)*

*If preferred, the dominant 7th may be finished on the starting note rather than resolving onto the tonic.

48

A major scale (to 12th)

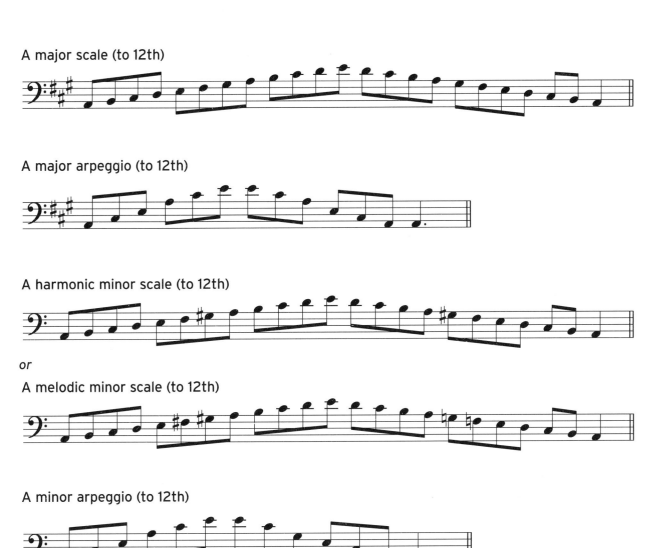

A major arpeggio (to 12th)

A harmonic minor scale (to 12th)

or

A melodic minor scale (to 12th)

A minor arpeggio (to 12th)

or ii) **Exercises:**

The following exercises to be performed *either* tongued *or* including legato as indicated, as requested by the examiner (♩ = 66-112):

A major scale and arpeggio exercise

Grade 5 continued

A minor scale and arpeggio exercise

F major expanding scale exercise

F minor expanding scale exercise

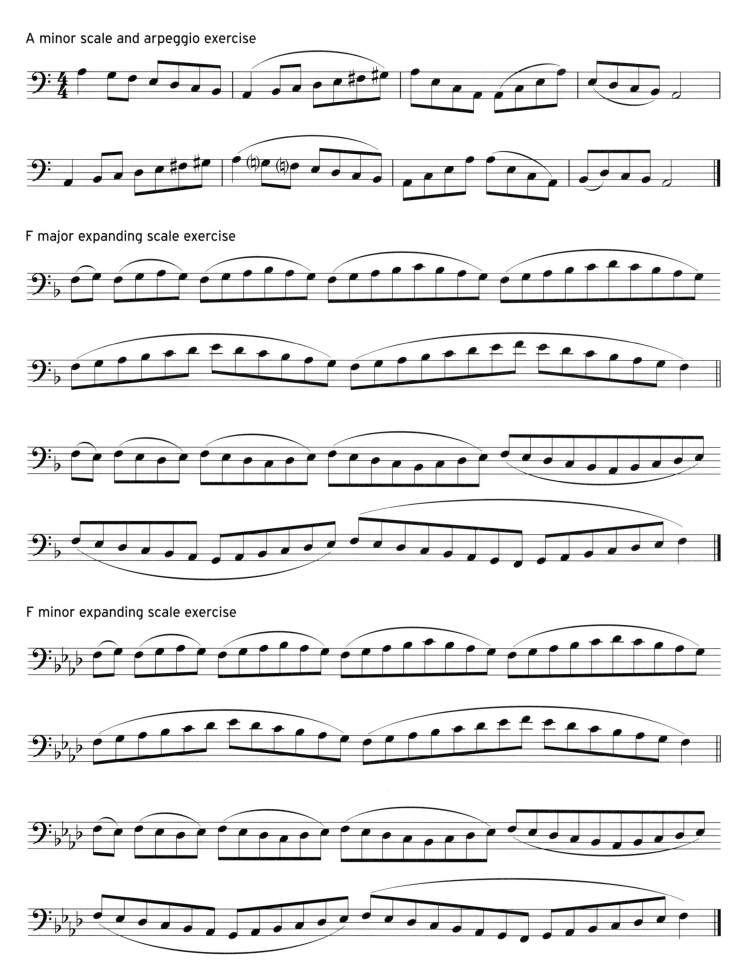

Grade 6

Candidate to prepare one lip flexibility exercise and then *either* Section i) *or* Section ii) in full:

Lip Flexibility Exercise:

No. 1 Ascending

♩= c. 160   Play this exercise legato, using the slide positions given.

Repeat using the following slide positions:

5th − 4th − 3rd − 2nd − 1st

or

No. 2 Descending

♩= c. 60   Play this exercise legato, using the slide positions given.

Repeat using the following slide positions:

2nd − 3rd − 4th − 5th −6th

either i) **Scales and Arpeggios (from memory):**

The following scales and arpeggios to be performed *f* or *p*, tongued *or* legato tongued as requested by the examiner (♩ = 72-120):

E major scale (two octaves)

E major arpeggio (two octaves)

Grade 6 continued

E harmonic minor scale (two octaves)

E melodic minor scale (two octaves)

E minor arpeggio (two octaves)

G major scale (two octaves)

G major arpeggio (two octaves)

G harmonic minor scale (two octaves)

G melodic minor scale (two octaves)

G minor arpeggio (two octaves)

Chromatic scale starting on G (two octaves)

Whole-tone scale starting on G (two octaves)

Augmented arpeggio starting on G (two octaves)

Dominant 7th in the key of G (one octave)*

Diminished 7th starting on G (two octaves)

*If preferred, the dominant 7th may be finished on the starting note rather than resolving onto the tonic.

Grade 6 continued

or ii) **Exercises:**

The following exercises to be performed *either* tongued *or* including legato as indicated, as requested by the examiner (♩ = 72–120):

Key centre exercise in G

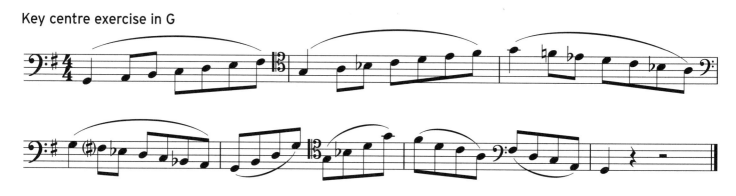

G major expanding scale exercise

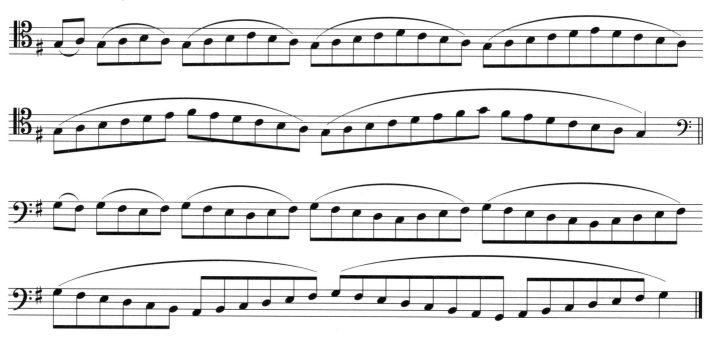

G major scale in thirds

G minor expanding scale exercise

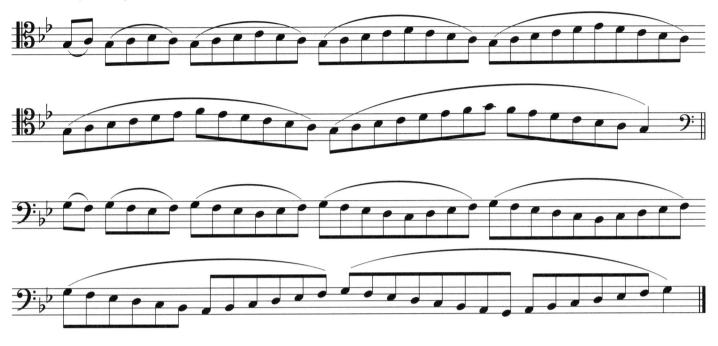

G minor scale in thirds

Grade 7

Candidate to prepare one lip flexibility exercise and then *either* Section i) *or* Section ii) in full:

Lip Flexibility Exercise:

No. 1 Ascending

♩ = c. 160   Play this exercise legato, using the slide positions given.

Repeat using the following slide positions:

5th − 4th − 3rd − 2nd

or

No. 2 Descending

♩ = c. 92   Play this exercise legato, using the slide positions given.

Repeat using the following slide positions:

2nd − 3rd − 4th − 5th − 6th

either i) **Scales and Arpeggios (from memory):**

The following scales and arpeggios to be performed $\boldsymbol{f}$ *or* $\boldsymbol{p}$, tongued *or* legto tongued as requested by the examiner
(♩ = 80-126):

A♭ major scale (two octaves)

A♭ major arpeggio (two octaves)

A♭ harmonic minor scale (two octaves)

A♭ melodic minor scale (two octaves)

A♭ minor arpeggio (two octaves)

Chromatic scale starting on A♭ (two octaves)

Whole-tone scale starting on A♭ (two octaves)

Grade 7 continued

Augmented arpeggio starting on A♭ (two octaves)

Dominant 7th in the key of A♭ (one octave)*

Diminished 7th starting on G♯/A♭ (two octaves)

A major scale (two octaves)

A major arpeggio (two octaves)

A harmonic minor scale (two octaves)

A melodic minor scale (two octaves)

A minor arpeggio (two octaves)

*If preferred, the dominant 7th may be finished on the starting note rather than resolving onto the tonic.

Chromatic scale starting on A (two octaves)

Whole-tone scale starting on A (two octaves)

Augmented arpeggio starting on A (two octaves)

Dominant 7th in the key of A (one octave)*

Diminished 7th starting on A (two octaves)

*If preferred, the dominant 7th may be finished on the starting note rather than resolving onto the tonic.

Grade 7 continued

or ii) **Exercises:**

The following exercises to be performed *either* tongued *or* including legato as indicated, as requested by the examiner
(♩ = 80-126):

Key centre exercise in A♭

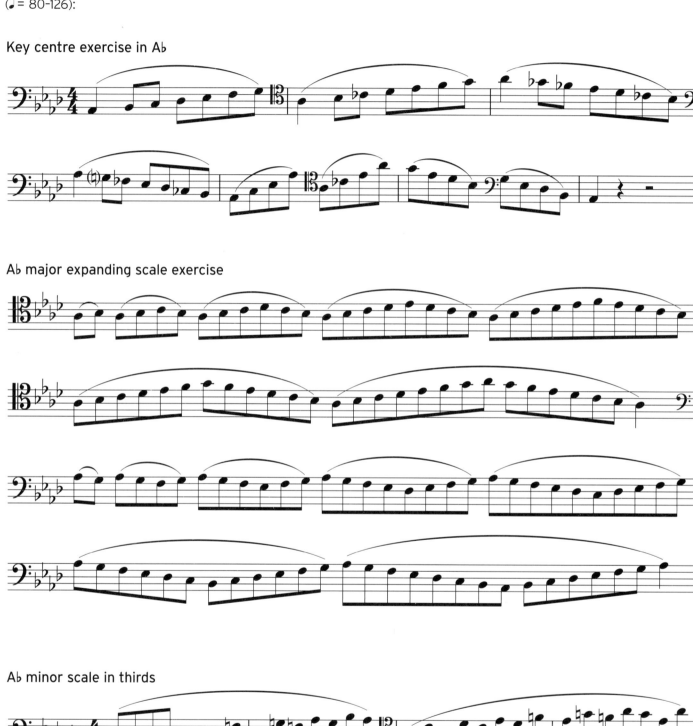

A♭ major expanding scale exercise

A♭ minor scale in thirds

A major scale in thirds

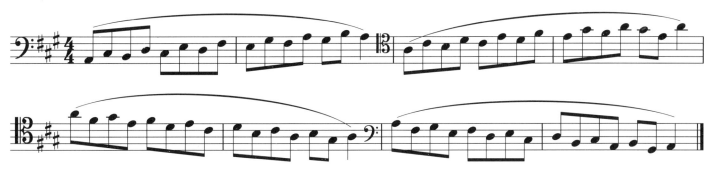

A minor expanding scale exercise

Grade 8

are one lip flexibility exercise and then *either* Section i) *or* Section ii) in full:

Lip Flexibility Exercise:

No. 1 Ascending

♩= c. 92   Play this exercise legato, using the slide positions given.

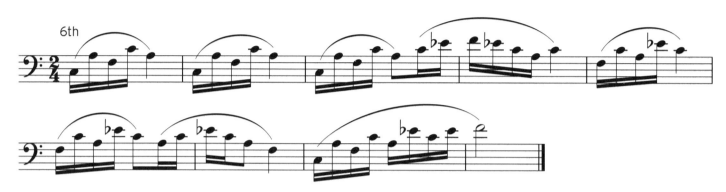

Repeat using the following slide positions:

5th − 4th − 3rd − 2nd − 1st

or

No. 2 Descending

♩= c. 92   Play this exercise legato, using the slide positions given.

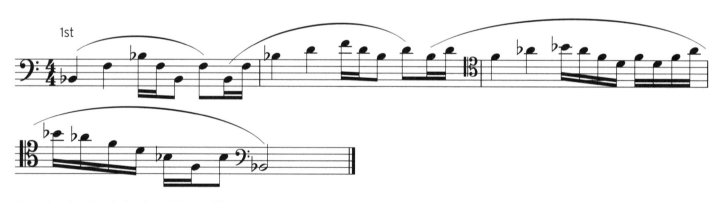

Repeat using the following slide positions:

2nd − 3rd − 4th − 5th − 6th

either i) **Scales and Arpeggios (from memory):**

The following scales and arpeggios to be performed $\boldsymbol{f}$ *or* $\boldsymbol{p}$, tongued *or* legato tongued *or* legato tongued in pairs (scales only) as requested by the examiner. ($\boldsymbol{\downarrow}$ = 88-132)

Bb major scale (two octaves)

Bb major arpeggio (two octaves)

Bb harmonic minor scale (two octaves)

Bb melodic minor scale (two octaves)

Bb minor arpeggio (two octaves)

Chromatic scale starting on Bb (two octaves)

Whole-tone scale starting on Bb (two octaves)

Grade 8 continued

Augmented arpeggio starting on B♭ (two octaves)

Dominant 7th in the key of B♭ (one octave)*

Diminished 7th starting on B♭ (two octaves)

E major scale (two octaves)

E major arpeggio (two octaves)

E harmonic minor scale (two octaves)

E melodic minor scale (two octaves)

E minor arpeggio (two octaves)

*If preferred, the dominant 7th may be finished on the starting note rather than resolving onto the tonic.

Chromatic scale starting on E (two octaves)

Whole-tone scale starting on E (two octaves)

Augmented arpeggio starting on E (two octaves)

Dominant 7th in the key of E (one octave)*

Diminished 7th starting on E (two octaves)

F# major scale (two octaves)

F# major arpeggio (two octaves)

*If preferred, the dominant 7th may be finished on the starting note rather than resolving onto the tonic.

Grade 8 continued

F# harmonic minor scale (two octaves)

F# melodic minor scale (two octaves)

F# minor arpeggio (two octaves)

Chromatic scale starting on F# (two octaves)

Whole-tone scale starting on F# (two octaves)

Augmented arpeggio starting on F# (two octaves)

Dominant 7th in the key of F# (one octave)*

*If preferred, the dominant 7th may be finished on the starting note rather than resolving onto the tonic.

Diminished 7th starting on F# (two octaves)

Crabwise scale from B♭ (two octaves - tongued *or* legato as indicated)

Crabwise scale from F (two octaves - tongued *or* legato as indicated)

Grade 8 continued

or ii) **Exercises:**

The following exercises to be performed *either* tongued *or* including legato as indicated, as requested by the examiner (♩ = 88-132):

Key centre exercise in B♭

Key centre exercise in E

Key centre exercise in F♯